# SURVIVING THE SINS

# WRATH

By

# C. A. King

Cover Design:
**SelfPubBookCovers.com/Ravenborn**
**Ravenborn Covers**

Editor: Editor: **Karen Hrdlicka**

*This book is dedicated to my Readers. Without you,
my novels would be nothing more than words on a blank page.*

*Look for other books by C.A. King, including:*

*The Portal Prophecies Series*

*Tomoiya's Story:*

*Book I: Escape to Darkness*
*Book II: Collecting Tears*

*Surviving the Sins:*

*Book I: Answering the Call*
*Book II: Pride*
*Book III: Lust*
*Book IV: Gluttony*

*When Leaves Fall: A Different Point of View Story*

*Peach Coloured Daisies: A Cursed by the Gods Story*

*Flower Shields: A Four Horsemen Novel*

*Drawing Strength From Words: A Four Horsemen Novel*

*Hitting The High Note: A Four Horsemen Novel*

*Miracles Not Included*

*Twisted Tales of A Dead End Street*

*Shot Through The Heart: A Faerie Tale*

*Do Not Open Until Halloween*

*Truly Unfortunate*

*Serendipity's Debt*

*Tails Always Wins*

*In a Heart Beat*

*Cupid's Connection*

Cover Design: SelfPubBookCovers.com/Ravenborn
Ravenborn Covers

*First Printing: April 29, 2019*

*ISBN: 978-1-988301-63-1*

*Kings Toe Publishing*
*kingstoepublishing@gmail.com*
*Burlington, Ontario. Canada*

# *Prologue*

*Balance* - the simple mention of the word has been known to invoke an image of a person walking on a tightrope, high above the ground, with no net. Each footstep would have to have been placed carefully; outstretched arms teetering up and down, back and forth. Falling was never an option. In a performance, the rope was a short distance, in life it never ended. It was that balance that made existence possible. To fail and tumble on either side could have been devastating. One trembling footstep steadied was the reason the next began to wobble. Cause and effect was a concept that should have been considered carefully by everyone. Unfortunately, it rarely was.

*The Portal Prophecies* may have saved the realms from Cornelius and Cornost, but by doing so, they opened doors to new problems at the same time. One could have said the metaphoric rope was shaken, its threads quivering. As a result, traversing it without tumbling became harder than it ever was before.

Change was inevitable in the Universe. A plant that sprouted from the ground as a tiny shoot grew into a blooming flower and, then withered away to seed. That very action brought new sprouts to life in the future. Some grew in the same spot, while others were whisked away by the wind to bring new scenery to lands previously untouched by their kind.

So, too, William's camp changed. The guardians were free to choose their own paths. Some returned to their homeland to help rebuild and others remained to establish new futures, choosing different keepers or to have none. The recently formed symbiotic relationships between two life forces weren't created without their share of problems. Something was lacking; perhaps the synergy or trust that had been taken for granted in the past.

The camp itself split in several different directions. One group headed home with the guardians to rebuild their world for future generations. Those who remained in the camp swore oaths to continue to defend the portals. The Shinning brothers,

Jessie, Dezi, and Pete, set out on a quest of their own to find a way to save their sister, Victoria, from the premature ageing that saving the lives of her family and friends caused her. Jade and Malarchy continued to forge a life in the political scene of the magical cities of the main world.

The forces that be searched for a new hero -- one was chosen.

An ancient god, Mornyx, sent out minions born of emotions to use certain individuals as puppets. Their purpose was not only to aid in Morynx's escape, but also to serve up the chosen mate on a silver platter; a child destined to be born from the union.

Jade was determined that neither herself nor anyone else would turn out to be the Chosen One. Together with a growing group of misfit friends, and a less-than-lucky leprechaun, she swore to stop Morynx's plans. With Pride, Lust, and Gluttony already having achieved success, she had only four more chances to save herself and the world...

# *An Excerpt From Lust*

Lucinda flopped onto the couch, letting out a loud huff. All the air she'd been holding in came out at once. Her strength had almost faltered in the presence of the man. Even now, she sat drained of composure. It could have been hunger, but more than likely lust was the culprit. She cursed under her breath at the thought of being desperate enough to use a poor excuse for a man as a mate.

A smile inched its way over her lips; a god looking to mate would be her salvation. She only needed to hold out a little while longer. This one she was taking for herself. What Mother didn't know, wouldn't hurt her.

Her vision cleared of haze, locking onto a picture on the wall. A perfect treat for the taking, containing the satisfaction she needed to wait things out.

The frame broke in two, crashing to the ground: its prisoner released. The black of Lucinda's eyes doubled in size. She licked her lips. One hand reached down, picking up the young woman lying amidst the picture's ruins.

"Amelia," Lucinda hissed.

The woman's small frame shook. Years of imprisonment had brought about dreams of escape. Now, her fate was sealed. Her eyelids grew heavy.

Lucinda's lips pressed against Amelia's, sucking out every ounce of life force until all that was left was a thin shell and brittle bones. Amelia's throat turned to dust in her grasp; what was left of the rest of the woman shattered on the floor.

"Lucinda!" Drakondia exclaimed. "What have you done? You know to take an essence like this is forbidden. We are to eat as our fathers did. Only Mother feeds on a life force. You know what happened to Hilary and Lara." When she spoke, she revealed four pointed teeth in the front of her mouth and a thin forked tongue popped out every time she pronounced an *s* sound.

Lucinda's eyes narrowed. "I forgot to eat," she replied. "I was light-headed. Report me if you must."

Drakondia lowered her glance to the floor. "Never," she whispered. "I'll clean this up." She picked up the jacket from the floor. "Are you okay?"

"I feel better now," Lucinda cooed, rubbing her fingers against Drakondia's three-dimensional tattoo of a spider.

"But your jacket," Drakondia whispered, swaying slightly.

"My jacket?"

"You are never seen without your jacket on," Drakondia answered.

"I was hot," Lucinda explained, taking a seat on the couch.

Drakondia knelt at her feet. "And the man? There is talk there was a man here who you let go. You know Mother needs more mates." The jaundiced colour of her skin intensified with her concern over the increasingly complicated situation.

"What Mother doesn't know won't hurt her," Lucinda whispered. "I can trust you not to tell, can't I?"

Drakondia rocked on the floor, mumbling gibberish mixed together with the occasional, "Mother knows best."

"Besides, the man was Hilary's lackey," Lucinda snapped. "He is still of use to us. In fact, I am going to go follow up with him in Pewterclaw."

"You?!" Drakondia shrieked. "You never leave here. Why are you not sending another team?"

"Not this time, Drakondia," Lucinda purred, petting her admirer's short, curly black hair while carefully avoiding the front part. It was spiked up as if it had been soaked in glue before walking headfirst into a hurricane-strength wind and as sharp as it looked. "This is far too important. It could change everything. I need to be the one to go."

"I'll join you," Drakondia offered. Her black eyes widened; two hot pits of tar, bubbling as steam escaped from within. There was absolutely no sign of any white in them at all -- or any eyelashes -- for that matter.

"I'm afraid not, my pet," Lucinda answered. "I need you here to keep things under control while I am gone. There are far too many looking for an opportunity to move up in The Organization. They would usurp my position in a second, given the chance."

"What would you have me do?" Every curl stood at attention along her hairline and never once moved, awaiting instruction.

Lucinda's lips curled up at the sides. "You can start by cleaning up this mess."

Drakondia hurried to comply, making sure there would be no traces found of Amelia's remains. A part of her was satisfied the woman from the picture prison was gone. Far too long Amelia had been Lucinda's favourite pet: a position that was meant only for herself.

# *Chapter One*

Drakondia caressed the three-dimensional spider tattoo heaving up and down with her every breath. She mumbled to it, as any good pet owner would, pacing the length of the room. There had been a few too many glares in the hallways and deceptive whispers in the walls. A bee named Gossip had been set free and its buzz was ten times more deadly than its sting. At this rate, she'd never be able to keep up the facade that all was as it should be.

Lucinda had been gone far too long. If she didn't return soon, a new leader would assume control of The Organization and Mother. The thought of such a vile betrayal made the venom pulsing through her veins boil.

Her thin forked tongue darted out, feeling the deception closing in. They were coming and it was even sooner than she had anticipated.

Her jaw dropped. Shallow breaths transformed into wild pants of anticipation. A piercing scream erupted from the depths of her mind, body, and soul; its volume breaking any glass it reached. The unleashed fury of the wind outside accepted the calling as a personal challenge. A test of power was afoot. Mother Nature fought back against the abomination she was. A gusty tempest took aim at the shattered windows, blowing shredded curtains wildly about behind her.

Drakondia prepared herself for a second toe-curling release, hoping the noise would keep usurpers at bay. A sharp pain on her shoulder had other plans, distracting her just long enough to give would-be traitors lurking in the dark the upper hand.

"I hope you didn't cut yourself too deeply," a mischievous voice said. "Didn't Mother tell you... you should be careful when playing with glass? Another loss for the family would be unbearable. Especially with all we have gone through as of late." If her words had a face it would have been pouting.

"Clementine," Drakondia blurted out, her voice stern. The palm of her hand slapped against her upper arm, attempting to steady its quivering. Dying was preferred to showing weakness. A small cut from a shard of glass or two was merely a pinch to her kind. "I'll be fine. What do you want?"

"You already know the answer to that," Clementine snickered. Her tongue became an artist's paint-brush; licking a smile onto her face. "Did you think we wouldn't notice you covering for Lucinda all this time? You know Mother doesn't like secrets. When were you going to share her whereabouts with the collective?" She circled her prey; stalking from the outskirts of the room. It wasn't time to pounce just yet.

Drakondia glanced away. "Lucinda had some important business to attend to. She should be returning at any moment. I have her blessings to act in her stead." A sly smile crept over her lips. A wild fire had been lit, bringing life to her otherwise dead eyes. They were two pits of tar without so much as a dot of white, or other colour for that matter. "Last I checked, she outranked you. Her instructions reign supreme until either she comes home or Mother decides otherwise."

"She's dead," Clementine blurted out.

"Lies," Drakondia hissed, her mouth dripping with contempt. "The lengths you would stoop to for power are truly frightening. In any other situation, I might have actually applauded you for such a vile deception. We both know, however, Lucinda is far too intelligent and powerful to succumb to anyone other than Mother herself."

"Foolish trollop! Your misplaced idolization has clouded your mind!" Clementine bellowed. "Your gifts have become weak. Forget the pedestal you place her on for a moment and reach deep inside. The answer is there. I know it, Mother knows it, and it's time you did as well. Lucinda is not coming back."

"Tricks!" Drakondia screamed. "You have always been jealous of her connection with Mother. If you think I'll step aside to let you waltz in and take over..."

Clementine cackled wildly. "Poor Drakondia, your allegiance has been misplaced for so long. What makes you think I need you to step aside? I came here as a courtesy to you, nothing more. The decision has already been made. Mother has spoken. With Lucinda dead, you best find a new owner to call you pet."

"She's not dead," Drakondia insisted. "I'll prove it. I'll find her, and when we return, you'll be sorry."

Clementine huffed a sigh, motioning a wave through the air with one hand. "Do what you must. I have no desire to continue this foolish conversation. Your idol left Mother without a suitable mate, and her appetite is reaching an insatiable level. I have no spare time to play with your foolishness. Heed this warning though: if you venture out into the world, no aid will be sent when you face the same end as your precious mistress."

Drakondia's eyes widened, watching the path Clementine took long after her physical form vanished. A forked tongue darted out, tasting what destiny held in store for her. The sweet tang only revenge could offer was on the menu for the foreseeable future. It was a good thing that had always been her favourite.

She returned her attention to the broken window. Even the wind had retreated, frightened by the pure rage growing within the belly of the beast. Her resolve promised to remain unwavering in the face of danger. Wrath demanded satisfaction, but Lucinda's well-being was first and foremost in Drakondia's mind.

# Chapter Two

Things had changed, but the eerie feeling that accompanied every trip inside the cave was not one of them. Even with Kasper's team hard at work, attempting to uncover the secrets that lay within the seals, Gavin's inner self screamed warnings to run the other way. Majesta, however, had won his curiosity.

The threat of a cave-in looming overhead didn't sway the artifacts specialist's resolve. Fear had no place in either her actions or voice when it came to her work. Majesta placed her faith in the magics that kept a collapse at bay and never once did it falter. Such bravery was a rare treat to find in any realm and deserved further observation.

"I brought you some food," Gavin offered, setting a tray down on a flat rock. "Are you sure you are comfortable staying in here alone?"

"It's fine," Majesta answered, prying the front of her shirt from where it clung to patches of skin. Even her short blonde hair proved to be fairing no better than her clothing, adhering to the sides of her face, drenched in salty droplets.

Humidity was an entity of its own. The temperature might have been a few degrees cooler inside the cave, but that translated into zero difference when inhaling thick moisture-laden air. With no breeze, there was no relief from the heaviness. Even overnight lows were well above that which the rest of the realm was experiencing.

That evening proved no different. All races were potential victims when it came to the suffering which weather patterns held the ability to inflict. That was the price paid for sporting physical forms. Trade-offs were inevitable. Good always came served with a side order of bad.

For most women, sweat was an appearance killer that led to disasters in the form of running makeup and frizzing dos. The young ancient artifacts specialist was an exception to that rule. On her, perspiration beaded like fine condensation on a cold glass, leaving a glossy shine behind that gave her complexion a healthy glow.

The food tray remained untouched, becoming nothing more than a token offering at a god's shrine. Majesta quietly resumed her work excavating the site. This was a crucial stage; no mistakes could be made.

Everything she needed had been placed within reach. An array of tools lay at the ready by her feet. Shovels and mattocks meticulously formed rows from smallest to largest, resting against rock. On the other side of her, brushes housed in a cloth pocket were kept within reach. Several wheelbarrows of dirt sat off to the side, awaiting relocation.

Gavin leaned against an empty wall. There was no reason to remain. Any presence was bound to serve as an obstacle placed directly in the woman's path. Distractions were the bane of any project. He knew that better than anyone. His thought shifted to a memory of Jade attempting to win his attention while conducting crucial experiments. A sigh escaped his lips. He should have left with it. The fact he didn't weighed heavy on his mind.

Majesta wasn't the most beautiful woman he had ever seen, but she seemed to hit all the right buttons. At first, it was the determined smile permanently etched on her face, displaying to the world her love of hard work. Then, sparked passion twinkling in her eyes caught his attention. He'd seen that intensity only once before... in a pair of icy green eyes. It was the same glimmer that drew him to another.

Jade's drive deserted her when her friends returned to their homeworld to rebuild it and hadn't made an appearance since. A part of him had mourned ever since; longing for any indication that sparkle would one day twinkle brightly again.

His heart fluttered, but for whom? The woman who first displayed a glistening view of the sheer devotion captured in her soul, or the one standing a mere four feet away. That was one answer that wasn't going to be found easily.

Neither his mind nor spirit deserved domain over such a choice. Conflict tore through him, feasting on indecision. His thoughts eagerly desired the power to inflict their influence over matters of the heart: a place where rational thought had no business sticking its nose.

Jade was drifting further away with every turn of the dial and Majesta was inching closer. Absence didn't make the heart grown fonder, common purpose did. The woman in front of him embraced what was inside the crevice, wanting to help uncover the truth. Their paths connected, magnets attracting them together. In the same way Jade was being driven beyond his reach. Still, a part of him longed to follow her through eternity.

Gavin stood, rubbing the back of his neck. "I'll leave you to it, then."

Majesta's smile grew exponentially. "Feel free to visit anytime. I'm not going anywhere anytime soon."

"You have work to do," Gavin replied. "But thank you for the offer."

"Nonsense!" Majesta exclaimed. "I am happy to listen if you ever need a friendly ear. This must be a troubled time for you. I get it. Hope is as deadly as any sin."

Gavin's lips curled up for the first time since arriving at the scene. "Maybe next time. I have to come back to bring you food and water... and check on your progress."

Majesta glanced up. "That's perfect. By tomorrow I expect to have some new information. I'm on the verge of discovering something huge. I can feel it breathing life into the rocks." She placed her ear against a wall, listening for the mountain's pulse.

"I have no choice but to come back now," Gavin admitted. "Anticipation makes for sleepless nights."

# Chapter Three

Toby took stock of what offerings the desk held for a little fella. Being inches tall made finding suitable furniture options in the main world difficult, to say the least. He chose a stack of papers to make a bed from. With an eraser behind his head, Toby lay back, legs bent with one knee crossed over the other. Comfortable, it wasn't. There was, however, nothing finer than watching a beautiful woman from the side. Jade made everything worthwhile. If only he could get rid of the other riff-raff hanging about and ruining a perfectly good day of daydreaming.

"Tell me again why you are in cluttering up my office," Jade complained. "I am sure there are plenty of other places for you to play with that thing."

"It's not a toy," Joseph argued. "It's a locking mechanism I desperately need to open." He shook the box, teeth grinding. "And I am here because the lot of you seem to be the only ones who might have a clue as to how it works."

"I have no clue," Simon admitted. "I spent an hour last night trying to find information on it."

"Ow!" Joseph complained. "It bit me!" He formed a fist, threatening the wooden box with violence for its actions.

"Priceless!" Toby exclaimed, falling off a stack of papers. He rolled from side to side, howling a laugh that echoed throughout the building. A tear streaked down reddened cheeks as he calmed himself into a sitting position. A single glance at the former prince was enough to start another round of hysterics. He slapped his knee, gasping for air.

"What," Joseph asked, "pray tell, is so funny?" His lips pursed together, fusing into a solid line.

"You," Toby stuttered amidst chuckles. "That isn't a normal puzzle box."

"What do you mean, not normal?" Simon asked, glancing up from a magazine that had caught his attention. "Have you seen this design before?"

"I'd like to know as well," Prudance declared, pushing Simon out of the way to claim her rightful place in the chair beside his brother.

"Please feel free to join us," Jade scoffed, tossing her pencil in the air. It landed dangerously close to the leprechaun's head. "It's not as if I have work to do. That contraption is obviously much more important."

"It's a cursed puzzle," Toby explained, wiping the last of the sweat from his brow. "Whoever gave it to you to solve isn't particularly fond of you."

"Okay," Jade conceded. "Now you have my attention as well. Explain. What did Kasper do to it?"

"There isn't much fer me to explain," Toby admitted. "It wasn't the director who enchanted it, albeit the puzzle has a magic attached to it. It was created to solicit a specific response. It was created for the sheer purpose of breaking the will of anyone who might find it."

"Break their will how?" Prudance questioned. "Puzzles are made to be difficult, but not impossible. Are you saying there is no solution?"

"Not at all," Toby replied, snickering. "This type of device was made to punish failure. Each time a person tries to solve it and is unsuccessful, it lashes out... hurting them. The pain level of the attacks increases with every attempt. By the time night falls, ye might be missing a finger or two if you aren't careful."

"That's barbaric!" Jade exclaimed.

"It wasn't me kind that came up with it," Toby stated. "They were made popular in medieval times by frightened witches and wizards. Things were a wee bit tough back then, even for the most magically adept. Hiding places were necessary for certain treasures, but good ones were few and far between."

"What could be so important that it would need a torture chamber to keep it safe?" Jade questioned, shaking her head. "I don't understand."

"Secrets," Toby hissed, his face shadowed by crimes of the past. "Everyone had them, and at that time, they could get a lass or lad killed. Magic wasn't an accepted practice, but games of the mind were. There was no better place to stow away precious amulets and potions than in a box, that to open, one faced the potential of death. That was an important part of our history. It was only a few full moons after that the empyral community decided to keep all magic a secret; hidden from those who couldn't understand it."

"Thanks for the history lesson, but all I really care about is finding a way to solve it," Joseph snarled. "Preferably without losing any body parts."

"That isn't any easy task," Toby declared. "At least not fer one person on their own. I'll give ye a hint, though. Spreading things out makes any task a wee bit easier. Do ye have enough friends willing to take a bit of pain?"

"I think I understand!" Jade exclaimed. "A person who was friendless wouldn't be able to solve the puzzle. Only those who were well liked could. Presumably, if you had enough friends willing to take a nip or two on your behalf, you weren't a threat to the contents or their owner."

"A lass after me own heart," Toby said. "Smart and beautiful."

"That's enough flirting," Simon scoffed. "Do you know the solution to this puzzle, or not?"

"I might," Toby answered, a sly smile twitching in the corners of his lips.

"So," Joseph complained. "Spill it, short-stuff. What is it? I need my wand."

Toby's tone turned dark. "There's only one way I'd reveal that to the likes of you."

"Please don't leave us hanging," Joseph snapped. "The suspense is too much to bear."

"Jade must use one of her wishes," Toby announced. "Only then will I teach you the answer you seek."

"That's not going to happen," Malarchy declared. "I knew the bout of laughter echoing through the halls meant our little leprechaun was up to no good."

"Mr. Mayor." Toby bowed at the waist. "You wound me with your words."

"I doubt that," Malarchy scoffed. "There will be no wishing by my daughter. I thought I made that clear. I don't trust you. There's a reason why you showed up when all of this started. Eventually we'll all know the truth, one way or another."

"Ye can't blame a fella for trying," Toby snickered. "Perhaps, since you are here, you can assist the prince in opening his puzzle."

Malarchy glared at Joseph. "That's not going to happen. Those who made the contraption had the right idea, making the lock based on trust. The truly evil will never be able to find the correct combination. I must remember to offer my praise to Kasper, next time I see him."

"Enough bickering!" Jade bellowed. "If you want to continue this conversation, I suggest doing it some place other than my office. I have enough to worry about without the lot of you adding to it."

Malarchy's lips puckered. "I'll be in my office, if you need me. Might I remind you, there is still a plot afoot. We all need to keep our wits about us."

"Perhaps we should concentrate on the next sin," Jade suggested, lowering her voice.

"Or perhaps one of them is already upon us," Prudance said. "Tempers are running rabid. Wrath is only a few steps away from anger."

Joseph huffed, "If wrath is what you are looking for, it's everywhere. Narrowing it down to the correct person will prove as difficult as solving this puzzle. You'll need all the help you can get. I am barely of use to you without my wand. Just a little food for thought."

Malarchy glanced back over his shoulder from the door. As much as he hated to admit it, the prince had a valid argument. Without his wand, Joseph was as useless as a water-soaked log thrown on a fire. The time might come when the prince's assistance might be needed; no matter what evils he did in the past.

# Chapter Four

Getting into Pewterclaw was a much easier task than Drakondia expected. All that left for her to do was to find the illusive moustache man. Luckily, his stint with Hilary had made him fairly well known, at least enough that loose lips were willing to gossip about his recent arrest. Pewterclaw jail was now the place the man hailed home. Ironically, a cell wasn't the preferred location for the interrogation she had in mind. There were far too many anti-illusion spells in effect whenever the police were involved.

Drakondia cackled. A jailbreak was just what she needed to take the edge off her nerves. Plotting and preparing eased the mind. A sharp pain in her midsection forced her to bow, acknowledging its existence before demanding a cure. Inflicting pain on someone else was the only one it was willing to accept.

City hall was unusually quiet for the middle of the day. An eerie haze, that usually only dreams were made of, fell over her eyes like a widow's veil. Shadowed in illusion, her feet glided forward with caution, unsure if a trap awaited them round the next bend.

The hairs on her spider tattoo stood on end, warning her of a possible ambush. The noticeably absent hustle and bustle, which should have existed in any government building, wasn't to be taken lightly. In a fair fight she could best the most magically adept. Being blindsided in a surprise attack, however, was another story. Only once before had she let her guard down. That fight ended in the loss of her teaching position at Sleeping Sands.

A piercing clamour sent waves of pain splintering through her mind. Some noises didn't deserve a wavelength from which to be heard.

"A leprechaun's laughter is never a good omen," Drakondia muttered to herself. "It does, however, provide ample cover for sneaking about." A grin formed spikes at the corner of her lips, sharper than any sounds a leprechaun could muster. They had proven formidable opponents in the past, but never a match for her illusions.

The absent employees made sense now. They were chasing a pot of gold at the end of a rainbow. With the front desk left unattended, there was no need for violence or illusions. Lucinda loved a good waltz. Music echoed within the confines of Drakondia's mind as she danced her way up the stairs that lead to the police department.

Boredom stoked the fires burning within. Finding officers put a skip in her step and an unnerving smile on her face. Not even an ounce of hesitation dared make an appearance.

"Can I help you?" one officer questioned. He glanced over her attire, noting every detail to no doubt enter in some report later that day.

"I need to speak with Safron Black," Drakondia demanded. "I'll wait while you fetch him."

The two officers exchanged glances and shoulder shrugs. "I am afraid Safron Black isn't allowed visitors."

"I see," Drakondia replied. "Is there someone higher up on the food chain I can speak with?" Her foot tapped, each bang against the floor becoming noticeable louder: a drum solo that was never meant for public ears.

"Sorry, ma'am," the officer answered. "You can come back tomorrow. The constable should be in then. We have our instructions. Mr. Black is not to have any outside visitors."

"It's just you two on duty? Imagine that," Drakondia snickered. "A skeleton crew on duty precisely at the same time that I happen to be famished." Her forked tongue darted out, leaving a layer of moisture glistening on her lips. Venom spewed from her mouth, melting anything it touched along the way. "Don't worry yourselves about trying to move. I'll let myself in."

A handful of tenderized flesh was more than enough of a snack to tide her over. Interrogation was, after all, a nasty business, bound to illicit an hefty appetite. She wandered past, wiping her feet on the carpet. A hole in the wall that led to the jail cells briefly halted her procession.

"Huh," Drakondia muttered. "I wonder whose handiwork that is." She shrugged her shoulders, the thought vanishing. Whoever laid waste to the wall was powerful, but long gone. Safron Black, however, was waiting on the other side.

The twinge of pain grew stronger, making her question if she was taking the right path. She snarled with determination, forcibly removing other obstacles from her mind. The man was her only lead to Lucinda and that was her only concern.

Agony ripped through her, forcing her to take a knee. That was the most she would give any unseen opponent, even if they did claim to be on the same side. She had her own strategy and was willing to do what it took to counter any moves made. Whatever game had been set afoot; she would be the one to reign victorious.

# Chapter Five

"Move," Drakondia demanded, poking her captive in the back with a crooked black wand. His lethargic movements weighed heavy on her demeanour. A throaty snarl escaped slightly parted lips.

"What is the meaning of this?!" Safron shrieked. One hand played double duty, hiding a gasp and stopping a heave from turning into a pile of vomit at the same time. The nauseous stench that had wafted in after the woman was unbearable. "Where is everyone?"

"I don't have time for your games," Drakondia screeched. "Did you really think shaving that moustache was going to hide you? I could taste your foulness from the moment I stepped foot in the city. It is undeniably the same as when you visited us." Her forked tongue darted out from between two fangs.

"Hide me from what?" Safron questioned. "You found me in jail. Obviously that isn't hiding." His finger rubbed gently over his upper lip. Only a bit of fuzz had returned since the leprechaun ruined his prized moustache. One day, revenge would be his, if the opportunity so arose. There was no need to go out of his way to find more trouble than he already had. Lately, more than his fair share of problems seemed to follow him everywhere he went.

"Just keep moving!" Drakondia ordered, one arm grasping her side. "You'll answer my questions once we are in a better location."

"My dear lady," Safron started.

"Silence!" Drakondia bellowed. "My tongue was designed to taste lies. Yours are particularly salty. Men are all the same: distasteful in every way. "

The tip of a wand pierced into his back. The pain didn't register, though. Bile from the deepest pit of his stomach found its way to his taste buds, stealing his attention. He gulped it back, begging it to stay put. One hand rose back to the site of the missing hair. If his moustache had still been there, it would have been filled with the finest perfumes. Without it, he was forced to endure the worst of scents. This odour, however, took the prize for the most putrid.

"What the devil happened here?" he asked, staring at the piles of melting flesh and bone. Never in all his years as constable had he seen such a mess. Hilary had been evil, but at least she was discreet about her indiscretions.

"I happened to them," Drakondia whispered in his ear. Her breath summoned the attention of the hairs on the back of his neck. "If you don't do exactly as I say, the same fate awaits you. Do we understand each other?"

A lump formed in Safron's throat. He swallowed it back together with all the moisture left in his mouth. A nod was all he could manage. One foot stepped over the first pile, avoiding coming in contact with sizzling steam.

"There must have been a better way," Safron cried. "Did they have to come to such a...sticky end?"

"Of course not," Drakondia cackled. "I am an expert at illusions."

"Then why?"

"Because, I decided I shouldn't be the only one suffering in pain," Drakondia hissed. "What is it people like to say... sharing is caring?"

"I'm not sure that is what that saying is referring to," Safron mumbled under his breath.

"As invigorating as this jailbreak is," Drakondia started, "it isn't enough to ease my calling. I suggest we move quickly. A pot boiling doesn't wait for anyone to overflow."

Safron's eyes shifted from side to side. The building was undeniably empty. Still, the crazed woman was leading him to the street. There were bound to be witnesses to call upon for help outside. Then, he'd make an escape plan on the fly.

The Organization might have come for answers, but what they accomplished was merely to set him free. It was a hop, skip, and a jump to reach a terunji city and hide out after ditching the yellow hag. This was working out better than if he had planned it himself.

# Chapter Six

Malarchy slumped back in his chair. His superheroesque appearance to save his daughter from the evil leprechaun hadn't gone quite as planned. It never did. For some reason a six-inch pain in the butt had managed to out wit him once again. Even if she scolded them both, Tobias was the one who remained by her side while he, her father, was excommunicated from her sight to the confines of his own office.

A deep breath refreshed his perseverance. There was other work to attend to. His chair rolled him closer to the desk. Pen in hand, he began a daily ritual of reading and signing. That was the boring and most prevalent part of being a mayor.

A knock on the door ended in a thump. Malarchy let out a huff, "Come."

"Sorry to disturb," Stan said, peeking his head round the corner.

The stench of death preceded the constable, making further concentration impossible. Malarchy pulled open a side drawer. A case of cardboard tree-shaped air fresheners, intended for use in cars, landed on the desk.

"I believe you enjoy the scent of pine," Malarchy said. He glanced up for the first time.

It was difficult, at best, to look directly at the constable on most occasions. His eyes pointing in opposite directions could throw even the most socially adept off. There was, however, one thing even harder; connecting glances with the man when one was missing.

As disgusting as it was, it was also mesmerizing. An empty socket glared back at him, some form of an insect wiggling around where an eyeball should have been.

"Did you lose something?" Malarchy questioned, dropping his pen.

"Oh, that," Stan replied. "It fell out this morning. I do need to speak to you, though. It's a rather pressing matter." His hands twisted a cap in unnatural ways.

"I'm sure it can wait until you find your missing eye and put it back where it belongs," Malarchy replied, ripping open the plastic on one of the air fresheners. "Here." His extended arm remained steady with the offering.

"Yes," Stan started, "about that. It isn't coming back. It fell into a pile of ooze and melted on contact."

"Ooze?" Malarchy questioned, one eyebrow arched in anticipation of the response. "Where exactly is this ooze you speak of?"

"W-well, u-um," Stan stuttered, tilting his head toward the ceiling. "It's upstairs."

"In the police department?" Malarchy asked. "I thought we went through the rules. No dangerous substances are allowed on the premises."

"I totally agree," Stan admitted. "Except, I didn't put it there. It's actually the rather messy remains of two of my men."

"Excuse me?!" Malarchy bellowed. "I thought I heard you say two officers were melted on city property. Tell me I'm wrong."

Stan nodded. "Sorry, but that is what it looks like. It's rather nasty business. It even smells worse than me." He picked up an air freshener. After examining the plastic it was sealed in, he held it out. "Would you mind? I've had enough mishaps for one day."

Malarchy made short work of the packaging. "Is there anything else I should know?"

"Well," Stan replied. "Safron Black seems to be missing from his cell."

Malarchy shook his head. "We rarely have prisoners, and yet when we do, they seem to always wind up missing or dead. Why is that?"

"I'm not sure, sir," Stand answered. "There is one more thing."

"What?" Malarchy asked through grinding teeth.

"I found the puddle remains on the floor," Stan said. "Upstairs."

"And?" Malarchy prodded, his hand making a circular motion. "Spit it out."

"And," Stan started, "it's a rather strong acid that appears to be responsible... one that eats through everything it comes in contact with. I haven't been able to find a way to clean it up as of yet."

"You want to close the department," Malarchy mumbled. "You can set up a temporary office in the old city hall by the hospital."

"It's a little more than just the department," Stan explained. "I need to evacuate the building."

Malarchy glanced up. "Is there a chance of it leaking through?"

"I'd say there is more than a chance, sir, " Stan answered. "It's only a matter of time. I need your authorization."

"Start with my daughter," Malarchy ordered, grabbing his jacket off the back of his chair. "I want her out of harms way before any panic sets in."

"Yes, sir," Stan replied, saluting.

"Then evacuate the building as quickly and quietly as possible. All non-essential employees are to take the rest of the day off. Everyone else will head to the old city hall. If anyone asks, it is merely a safety drill to test each of the departments preparedness."

"Got it," Stan agreed.

"And once you have things under control, go to the hospital's spare parts department and pick yourself up a replacement eyeball."

"Thank you, sir," Stan replied. "What about the mess upstairs?"

"I'm heading there now," Malarchy said. "If I can't control it, I'll have to call in Vern."

"The Director of Dangerous Substances?" Stan questioned. "Won't he wonder what happened?"

"Indeed," Malarchy muttered. "I'll tell him we were attacked, but it is under control. He won't want to alarm citizens any more than I do. Off you go. There's much to do."

# Chapter Seven

Majesta rolled her eyes at the sight of yet another tray of unappetizing food. It was slated for the same hole the ones that came before it had ended up in. The silver place setting clanged on the tray, empty of its contents. The brush in her hand shook. She would need to feed properly soon.

"Good afternoon," Gavin said. "I trust everything is going well."

"Yes," Majesta replied. "Look." She stood back, allowing the vampire a full view of the picture she was uncovering. That was enough to cover up her racing heart. He'd assume it was excitement from a new discovery rather than a by-product of being surprised by his sudden appearance. It wasn't like her to let anyone have the advantage of sneaking up from the rear.

Gavin squinted. "What is that?" he asked, tilting his head to the side."

"I believe it is a pile of treasure," Majesta replied, gold fever reflecting in her eyes. "It looks as if there was a payoff made for sealing Morynx in."

"I'm not sure that is good news," Gavin said, rubbing the back of his neck. "For any god to be considered evil enough to warrant putting a contract on his head..."

"You are looking at it all wrong," Majesta argued. "I believe someone evil wanted Morynx out of the way. Your ancestor was buried in rock and stone out of sheer greed."

"But why?" Gavin asked.

"I would have thought you, above all, would understand," Majesta replied. "The terunji and even the empyral of this world are easily frightened by that which they know nothing of and understand even less about. Prejudice is enough motive for murder."

Gavin nodded. "Yes," he agreed. "That has held true time and time again. Most people of this realm act first and ask questions later. If they are found to have been hasty, they chalk any consequences up to some notion that protecting the greater good is an entitlement to take action."

"I believe that is what happened here," Majesta said. "There are crude sketches all through the passages that support my theory. I'll need to go a tad farther in, though."

"It is too dangerous," Gavin argued. "None of us have even considered venturing farther into the mountain. I can't allow you to take that much risk under my watch."

"Send in Kasper's team," Majesta demanded. "I'll have them secure any area before I take a look-see." She smiled, reaching out to grasp his hand.

Gavin felt his head nodding. A simple squeeze was enough to make his resolve falter. Going farther into the passages was a mistake and he knew it. Still, he agreed despite his reservations. His eyes locked on their intertwined hands. His vision fogged over.

"Sorry," Gavin muttered. "What were you saying?"

"You look a bit off," Majesta declared. "This cave can be quite daunting. Why don't you send Kasper's men in?"

"Yeah," Gavin agreed, rubbing the back of his neck. "I'll tell them you need help." He glanced over his shoulder, bogged down with a nagging feeling that wool had somehow been pulled over his eyes.

# Chapter Eight

The door to salvation had been opened and Safron willingly barged right through. The street, however was empty. He spun around, looking for any sign of life. "What is this magic?!"

"Illusions are powerful things," Drakondia snickered. "Don't worry the good citizens of Pewterclaw are still here. You just can't see them, nor they you."

"How is this possible?!" Safron yelled.

"I assure you it is entirely safe," Drakondia declared. "If it would make you feel better, I could let you see what is going on around you."

"Yes," Safron begged. "That would be much better." He waited with bated breath.

Drakondia cackled, twirling around in a circle. The veil lifted, providing a view of everyday life, as it should be. "The spell makes you go around any obstacles so no collisions happen," she explained.

Safron waved his hands in front of one pedestrian on the sidewalk then another. They each simply walked around him as if he didn't exist. "Help!" he screamed.

"They can't hear you," Drakondia snarled. "I'm not daft enough to step you completely free. I merely gave you back your vision. This..." she motioned in a circle with one hand, "is an illusion bubble. We're both in it and only the two of us. You can yell and cry all you want. No one sees you and no one hears you other than yours truly."

"What do you want from me?" Safron questioned, his shoulders slouching in defeat.

"I want answers!" Drakondia demanded. "You came to see Lucinda... why?"

"I think there has been a big misunderstanding," Safron mumbled, waving his hands in front of his chest. He took a couple of steps backwards. "I was there looking for a job. Hilary had made some rather big promises..."

"Hilary," Drakondia repeated. "News flash... she's dead. In fact, didn't she die here in Pewterclaw?"

"Yes. Bad business, really. I worked for her and well... she offered me a position with The," Safron's voice lowered to a whisper, "Organization."

"You let her die and thought we would give you a job?" Drakondia questioned, pacing. "That's rather gutsy."

"Yes," Safron said, straightening his posture. "I like to think..."

Drakondia held up her hand. "And rather stupid."

"I believe the saying goes, when life gives you lemons," Safron replied, "everyone gets lemonade, or something like that."

"If life gave me lemons," Drakondia hissed, "I'd squirt them in the eyes of the one delivering them."

"I can see how that might be a viable interpretation," Safron agreed. "But it wasn't the one I was going for."

"You do realize," Drakondia continued, "in this scenario, you are the one delivering them."

"There is another saying I prefer." Safron's voice shook. A throaty cough fixed the problem. "Don't shoot the messenger."

"Why not?" Lucinda asked. "If the message has been delivered what good is he any more?"

Safron held up a single finger. His jaw dropped open as if it had something of great significance to say.

"Don't bother," Drakondia commanded. "I have no interest in further playing these games. Your stalling tactics are becoming bothersome. I want to know where Lucinda is and I want to know now."

"Lucinda," Safron repeated, gulping back pooling saliva. "Yes, well last time I saw her she was at a camp."

"Explain," Drakondia demanded, one finger lifting his chin so their eyes could meet. "Did you leave her to die as you did Hilary?"

"Not exactly," Safron answered. "Lucinda cocooned me and left me to die."

Drakondia howled a laugh that rivalled even the loudest of storms on the horizon. "What happened? I want all the details and I want them now."

"T-there r-really isn't m-much to t-tell," Safron admitted, a stutter forming in his words. "Lucinda showed up in much the same manner as you did. She was looking for information. Some rumours had been circulating about an imprisoned god named Morynx. Then there was some talk about having babies that I didn't understand. I only agreed to help her because she offered to uphold Hilary's previous agreement. You wouldn't be interested in making a similar proposal, would you?"

Drakondia's upper lip lifted, releasing a low snarl. "No, I most definitely wouldn't. I am getting hungry, though." Her forked tongue darted out between two fangs, licking the constable's cheek.

"Ah," Safron said, leaning as far away as possible. "I took her south; to the location of the camp where Morynx is thought to be jailed. That's when she cocooned me. The mayor and his entourage cut me out of the encasement hours later. It was brutal. They mocked me while I was frozen, allowing a leprechaun to shave off half of my moustache."

"What happened to Lucinda?" Drakondia barked. "Your facial hair has no relevance."

"I don't know," Safron admitted. "She went inside the cave. I never saw her again. I was arrested. No one around here was going to let me in on whatever happened that day."

Drakondia let out a shrill scream. "Take me there," she demanded. "Help me unravel the truth and I might let you live."

Safron nodded. "It's not like I am going to get a better offer," he said. "We'll need to make a few preparations."

"No!" Drakondia exclaimed. "We leave now. Lucinda must have been making arrangements for a new mate for Mother. She always thought of others before herself. That is why I loved her so much. If there is even a sliver of hope to cling to I must grasp it."

"Or we can leave now," Safron agreed. "I will warn you, though, it is hot in the jungle. There is also a camp of vampires protecting the area we'll need to get around."

Drakondia chuckled. "They won't even see us coming."

# Chapter Nine

"Thanks for heading over so quickly," Malarchy said, extending his hand. "The building has already been fully evacuated."

"Always glad to help," Vern answered, accepting the mayors offer to shake. "Besides, I have to admit I am a bit curious as to what the mayor would need with the Director of Dangerous Substances. What seems to be the issue?"

"I'm not entirely sure," Malarchy admitted. "It appears to be some sort of an acid. The stuff is eating through everything. Our cleanup crews can't even touch it."

"Acid?!" Vern exclaimed. "How in the realms would that end up in city hall?"

Malarchy shook his head. "I was hoping you could give me the answer to that. At least if I knew what it was, I might be able to figure out the rest of the puzzle."

"Are you quite sure the area is secure?" Vern asked. "I hate to think negative things, but it very well could be a terrorist attack."

"I thought of that, too," Malarchy replied. "I had Stan do a sweep and I have done one myself. I sense a bit of residual illusion magic lingering in the air, but nothing physical to worry about." He led the way up the stairs.

"My word," Vern muttered, taking off his hat and holding it over his heart. "You realize there is a residual amount of body bits mixed in there, don't you? You are dealing with more than an acid. At least one person has died."

Malarchy's lips pursed together. He nodded. "The two officers on duty at the time of the incident are missing. I was holding out hope that they weren't involved."

"Has Kasper been contacted?" Vern asked.

"Kasper is taking some time off after weathering an attack of his own," Malarchy replied. "It's just us to take care of the details of this mess."

"I don't like that," Vern mumbled, "not one bit." He affixed a pair of thick goggles around his head. Black gloves covered both hands, before pulling out a chemistry set. "Stand back, old man. I don't want to splash you by mistake. Unknown dangerous substances aren't an exact science, if you know what I mean."

"Indeed. I'd prefer not to have any melting my new suit, or something more important," Malarchy admitted, taking several large steps backwards.

A beaker scooped up some of the ooze. "This looks like ordinary glass," Vern said, holding up his prize to the light. "But it is enchanted. I don't have much time, though. I'll have to run the tests from here." He poured a sample into several different test tubes. Pulling out various other items from his kit, he added powders, papers, and dyes to each. His gloves snapped as they peeled off. "Hm."

"Don't leave me wondering!" Malarchy exclaimed. "What in the damned realms is it?"

"It appears to be a mixture of several things," Vern explained. "After I separated out the tissue of the victims, it left a rather odd combination of two deadly agents. I'm afraid if this means what I think it does, we have a problem on our hands that could prove to be bigger than either of our britches."

"Spit it out!" Malarchy demanded. "If it is as terrible as you say, there are innocent citizens in need of protection."

"The first agent is the venom of an achaear," Vern said. "We haven't actually come across the other before, but it is equally as destructive."

"What does this mean?" Malarchy asked.

"I believe we are dealing with a new hybrid," Vern suggested. "It may even be the only one of its kind. With the difficulty we had in the past with certain offspring of the ancients, this discovery leaves room for some concern."

"But what is it doing in Pewterclaw?" Malarchy questioned. "And why now?"

"That's the mystery, isn't it?" Vern packed up the unused portion of his kit. "I have a team on standby to clean this up for you, but I suggest the building remain quarantined for a few days to stay on the safe side."

"Thank you," Malarchy muttered, lost in his own thoughts. There had to be a connection to the sins. If he was right, Jade was in a new world of trouble. This foe was potentially stronger than anything else they had seen before.

# Chapter Ten

Jade stood back, taking in all the sights the ruckus going on around her was providing. Every department had been woefully unprepared for a disaster scenario, unless complete and total chaos was the intended result. Somehow she doubted it was.

No one knew what direction to take; no floor plan existed for offices to be set up. Even with half the staff sent home, crowds were banging heads everywhere she looked.

"Jade!" Jessica called out, waving one hand over top of the masses.

The voice came through crystal clear, but the face evaded her vision. She hopped up on her tiptoes for a better vantage point. Finding a lost diamond in a mountain of coal would have been easier and less messy.

If Gavin had been there, he would have picked her out in a heartbeat. He wasn't though and she didn't know if he ever would be again. The voices of her friends lecturing about her relationship with Gavin swarmed her thoughts. It was the first time she understood their words for what they truly meant. At that moment, however, she wished there were a few less fish in the sea. A tug on her arm pulled her into an empty office.

"This used to be the mayor's meeting room," Jessica said, tossing her bag on the table. "Hopefully the others will figure out we're in here."

"It's a madhouse out there," Jade muttered. "No one knows what to do."

"A total breakdown of communication," Joseph snickered. "I would have thought city hall and the mayors office would have been prepared for any emergency." The door remained open behind him. The puzzle box hit the table.

"Glad to see you have your priorities straight," Jade scoffed, rolling her eyes.

"Like it or not," Joseph replied. "The time will come when you need my magic to save the day. That can only happen if that contraption opens. So yes, I have my priorities straight. Do you?"

Jade opened her mouth. The force of a thousand wild horses was restrained by only one thing; her father's voice.

"STOP!" Malarchy bellowed. The crowd obeyed, freezing in their footsteps. "This test has already completely failed. In an emergency, the good citizens of Pewterclaw expect their city officials to keep their wits about them. We will continue to work from here until we achieve an undeniable success. The city hall we all know and love is on lock down until further notice."

"What are we supposed to do?" a man cried out. "Everything is inside our offices. Can't we retrieve our files? This is insane!"

"What would you do if this was an actual emergency and city hall didn't exist anymore?" Malarchy snapped back. "We need to be able to maintain a functioning government from any location. Department heads; find a room and set up. I expect to see business as usual within the hour." He jumped down from the desk he used as a stage and headed toward the open door that was beckoning him to enter.

"Great speech," Jessica praised. "So this is a test? I was concerned. Why did things fall apart? I thought we had contingency plans."

"We have a few key members of the team who are otherwise disposed of," Malarchy answered. "Esmerelda is off and there is no support coming from Kasper. Stan had a rather serious injury to attend to, as well."

"Injury?!" Jade exclaimed.

"He lost an eye and it was destroyed," Malarchy replied. "He should be picking out a new one at the medical centre as we speak."

"What should we do?" Jessica questioned.

Malarchy glanced around the table. "Gather supplies and the rest of the team. I have summoned the others we need for an important meeting. Once we are all here, I'll fill you in on the details."

"I take it there is more information on the illusive sins?" Joseph questioned, his brow arching.

"I don't recall you being a part of the team..."

"Enough, Jade!" Malarchy ordered. "We can use all the help we can get on this one."

"Is it that serious?" Jade asked, falling backward into a chair.

Malarchy's eyes dulled. "It is far more dangerous than anything we have seen before."

"Well then," Joseph said, scratching his head. "I'll find my brother and Prudance." Jessica closed the door behind them.

"I don't trust him," Jade said, locking her gaze on the puzzle. "How do we know he won't turn on us?"

"How did you know Simon wouldn't?" Malarchy asked, turning his back to the table.

"I guess I didn't," Jade said, a nervous chuckle tagging on the back end of her words. "I simply decided to give him another chance."

"Why?" Malarchy whispered, shoving one hand into the pocket of his pants.

Jade's eyes shifted from side to side, looking for an answer. "Jessica said..."

Malarchy spun around. "No!" he exclaimed. "It wasn't because of anything Jessica said. Oh, she brought him to you with the intention of helping, but you decided to let him help."

"He was the only one who could offer me assistance in the dream world," Jade muttered.

"Exactly, you needed him," Malarchy confirmed, snapping his fingers.

"What kind of a person does that make me?" Jade cried. "That's the worst reason to forgive someone."

"Forgiving Simon and trusting him to aid in solving an urgent problem are two different things," Malarchy explained. "You accepted his help long before you made up your mind to give him a second chance."

"You don't think the two coincide?" Jade questioned. "Regardless, I used him. That isn't right."

"You accepted his offer to help," Malarchy argued. "It started out as a one-time deal. Afterwards, when you saw he was, in fact, making an attempt to better himself, you had a change of heart."

"Is this situation with Joseph really comparable?" Jade asked. "He played a bigger role in our past than his brother. I am not sure the pain will ever disappear."

"I am only suggesting we let Joseph play a supporting role," Malarchy replied, turning around again. "Just this once. He'll either save the day or show his true colours. If there is one thing you should have taken away from dealing with all these sins, it's we all need to avoid them like the plague. Don't let pride interfere with things that are far more important. Survival I'd put at the top of that list."

"If he turns on us?" Jade muttered.

Malarchy's lips curled up. "Then we'll have every reason to destroy him."

"The puzzle..."

Malarchy spun around again, this time with a full snarky grin. "I see no reason to interfere, at the moment. I rather enjoy watching the young prince flounder."

# Chapter Eleven

Birds screamed from their perches hidden amongst the treetops. Animals were apparently unaffected by even the strongest of illusion magics.

"Are you sure we are going the right way?" she squawked, dabbing perspiration from her spider tattoo. "If you are trying to trick me..." Drakondia screeched, her voice sending all manner of animals running in fear. Thick leaves rustled, being trampled in the stampede.

"No tricks, my dear lady," Safron snickered. "I tried to warn you about the geographical area we were heading to." His wand cleared a path through the thick vegetation blocking the way. "I am but a guide. I have no control over the temperatures, or weather." He glanced over his shoulder, smirking. A black full-length sundress might have been a great way to showcase a tattoo or two, but wasn't an ideal outfit for hiking through a jungle. "You probably should have worn something a little more appropriate for this long an expedition."

"How far?" Drakondia barked. Aggravation was doing a number on her emotions. Anger was the only one she wanted. There would be a place and time for the others when all was said and done. Until then, focus was the name of the game. That was hard to do in sweltering heat.

Normally the spikes at the front of her short black hair could withstand anything, including a hurricane-strength wind. At that moment, however, it sagged -- individual curls dropping down over her eyes. For a woman with no lashes, that was a problem. Blinking wasn't something she enjoyed. The split second it took to fully close one's eyes and open them again was enough time for an enemy to seize the upper hand. Between sweat and rogue locks, there was little choice, though.

"Patience is a virtue," Safron hummed. "All good things come to those who wait."

"Being made to wait only serves as fuel for a burning rage," Drakondia hissed, the yellow tinge to her skin darkening. "And virtues I am always running out of. I don't see anywhere to restock, either. Why are we stopped?"

Safron stepped to the side. One finger extended, pointing toward an intricately spun web. "One of your own? I wouldn't want to hurt a close relative."

"Don't be ridiculous," Drakondia barked, rolling her eyes. "I am not sentimental about those who are weak, no matter what the race." She backhanded the spinner, destroying maker and web in one blow. "Move."

"As you wish," Safron agreed, bowing his head. "The camp is close. Did you want to make a plan after doing a bit of surveillance?"

"I told you before," Drakondia complained, "no one can see either of us. There is no need for sneaking about, pretending to be spies."

"Yes, well," Safron said, his eyes averted to his own feet, "perhaps you can let me in on the plan so I can further serve to direct you."

"I plan to go into the cave and find out what happened," Drakondia announced. "That is it."

Safron gulped back the lump forming in his throat enough to speak. "Into the cave," he squeaked. "It might be prudent for me to remain outside... to keep watch."

"If no one knows we are here," Drakondia scoffed, "why would we need a lookout?"

"Right," Safron muttered. His mind raced. There had to be another way to escape. All he needed was to keep his cool and come up with a new plan. A shiver raced down his spine at the thought of the vampires being his only hope. The last run-in with their kind hadn't gone well. His fingers instinctively ran over his upper lip again.

Throughout history there were tales of great men who owed every ounce of their power to hair. Safron's might not have been on the top of his head, but that moustache had been the source of his strength. Without it he was naked: vulnerable. The leprechaun hadn't just shaved off a prized possession; he'd stolen his tenacity. Without confidence, any man was reduced to no more than a helpless crying babe.

# Chapter Twelve

Stan came through the door first, tumbling in a way that was unusually clumsy even for him. "Sorry," he muttered, from a position hunched over the table. His body slid into a chair as if it were melting. The palm of his hand slapped against the side of his head several times.

"What happened to you?" Simon asked. "You look worse than your usual dead."

"I seem to be having a hard time adjusting to this new eye." He blinked several times. The latest addition wasn't a match to the older version, being an entirely different colour and facing forward.

"Purple," Joseph said, "interesting choice. How many fingers do you see?" His index digit moved back and forth in front of both of the constables eyes.

"Three," Stan replied. "I am pretty sure that isn't right, though."

"Normal adjustment is twenty-four to forty-eight hours," Jessica suggested. "Double vision isn't an uncommon side effect of such an acquisition. These adjustments take time."

"What about seeing things that aren't actually there?" Stan asked, moving his hand close to his face and away again.

"What sort of things?" Malarchy questioned.

"All sorts," Stan answered. "It comes and goes. I can see people sweeping in the corner." He nodded. Shooting out of his chair, his body shook, bits of decay falling off. "There are people sitting around the table, too."

"Hallucinations perhaps," Malarchy suggested.

"No," Miss Kelly disagreed from the door. "It is rather amusing to watch, though. Didn't you ask for a history of the part you were getting before accepting it?"

"No," Stand admitted. "I was in a hurry with all the commotion at city hall. Besides, I didn't know that was a thing. Do all body parts have histories?"

An unnerving cackle escaped from deep within the old hag's throat. Her staff banged against the floor.

"I believe we may have missed the punch line," Simon said. "Perhaps you could let us in on the joke."

"That right there," Miss Kelly said, pointing with a crooked finger at the replacement, "is a seer's eye. To answer your other question, yes. All body pieces have to come with a complete run-down of who they were owned by, any known diseases, and probability of match between species."

"Are you telling us Stan can see the future?" Malarchy blurted out.

"The future, the past... the different possibilities that were, are, and could be," Miss Kelly answered. "It will drive you mad if you don't get a handle on it. I am surprised you found one. They are a rare commodity."

"The parts department offered it to me," Stan explained. "I wasn't about to be fussy. Maybe it was a mistake. I could try to return it for a different one."

"That wouldn't be a wise decision," Miss Kelly warned. "The eye has already begun to fuse with you. To rip it out now could cause your essence to be torn apart at the same time. You are evolving."

"Evolving into what? I'm not sure I like the sounds of any of this. What should I do?" Stan questioned. "Everything is a blur. I can't even see straight enough to walk."

Miss Kelly reached into her pocket. "I was wondering why I needed to bring this along," An eye patch landed on the table between them. "This will help as you learn. You will need an instructor. There isn't much time if you are to keep your sanity intact."

"Can you help him?" Jade asked.

"I can," Miss Kelly replied. "It would take all of my time and effort, though. I fear your father has brought me here for a much different problem."

"Indeed," Malarchy admitted. A finger pressed against his lips. "But Stan come first." He sighed, "That leaves us short-handed, though."

"For what?" Prudance questioned.

"There is a new threat on the horizon," Malarchy said. "I fear it is going to take a group effort to survive this one. We've discovered a hybrid in Pewterclaw that we can't take lightly. By all accounts this will be our most difficult task to date."

"Shouldn't we hold off the classes, then?" Stan inquired. "I might not be the strongest to the lot, but my instructor could be of some use."

No," Malarchy said, waving him off. "You two need to get started. Hopefully, you'll be done by the time assistance is needed. We have no way of knowing when or where the next attack will take place, or if it will happen at all."

"Attack!" Jessica shrieked. "So this wasn't a trial run? Something actually happened?"

"Something actually happened," Malarchy repeated, staring off into the distance.

# Chapter Thirteen

Safron stopped short of the cave's mouth. "That's it," he whispered. "The last time I saw Lucinda, she was heading in there."

"You don't need to whisper," Drakondia huffed, pushing him to the ground. "No one will hear you unless I let them." She glanced over her shoulder after a nonchalant jaunt to the entrance. "Get off the ground and make yourself useful. It's dark in there. I need light."

Safron brushed himself off, grumbling a few choice words under his breath.

"I heard that," Drakondia complained. "Stop your griping and let's get this over with."

A torch in hand, Safron inched forward into the black. The light flickered, shaking along with his knees. One foot pushed a few pebbles loose; their movements echoed breaking the silence. Chattering teeth joined in. A gust of wind added its roar, upset at being blocked from entering along with them.

"Not afraid are you?" Drakondia snickered.

Her hot breath scorched his neck. Hairs stood at attention, but these soldiers wanted to run. They tugged at his skin to no avail. There was no escape for those rooted in place.

"BOO!" she screamed in his ear, cackling as he jumped. The torch fell, extinguishing the moment it hit the ground.

"I can relight it," Safron stuttered. He fumbled for his wand among the dirt and rock.

"Never mind," Drakondia ordered. "There seems to be enough of a glow up ahead. What is that?"

Without waiting for an answer, she left Safron behind. An orange brilliance beckoned her to a crack in the stone. The heart of the mountain was all but exposed.

"What are you doing here?" an eerie, disembodied voice called out. Power resonated in every syllable.

"I am looking for Lucinda," Drakondia replied, her determination refusing to falter. "What have you done with her?"

"The one you speak of is dead," the voice answered. "There is nothing you can do for her. Begone before a similar fate befalls you."

Drakondia let out a blood-curdling scream, dislodging dirt and gravel above. The shower greyed her hair and clothes. "Show yourself, god," she demanded. "Tell me your name and then I shall exact my revenge."

"Why don't I just wait for you outside?" Safron asked. "I can see you have everything under control here." Without waiting for permission, he turned and fled. None of this was what he signed up for. The Organization could keep their job. He wasn't suicidal.

"Foolish man..." Drakondia started.

"Do not concern yourself with that one. He is of no use to either of us. Focus on my words, my little puppet. I am Morynx. Wrath has for some reason led you astray," the voice explained. "This is not the place you are meant to be."

Drakondia's body swayed in time with the words. A caress lighter than a feather ran over her shoulder and arms. "Then tell me where my rage is best served."

"If you look deep inside, I believe you will find that answer," Morynx suggested. "If not, then perhaps glance down at your feet."

Drakondia squatted down. Her hands fumbled over a photograph. "Is this the one?"

"Yes, that is your target," Morynx answered. "Do you know who she is?"

"Tell me," Drakondia screeched. "Tell me and I shall make things right -- a life for a life."

"She came with others," Morynx said. "Find the mayor of Pewterclaw and you will find her. Go now, before your wrong turn causes any more glitches in my plans and I take issue with you. Win your battle and we shall both be released."

"I sensed a leprechaun in Pewterclaw," Drakondia stated. "How is that foul creature connected?"

"Don't worry about that creature," Morynx replied. "I have something very special planned for our little friend. Leave him to me."

"And if he gets in my way?" Drakondia questioned.

"Then kill him," Morynx ordered. "Just make sure the girl dies at the same time."

Drakondia's stride picked up speed. "With pleasure," she snarled without glancing back.

Majesta stepped out from the shadows. Each of her fingers took a turn pushing past her lips for a thorough cleaning. Things were about to become much more interesting.

# Chapter Fourteen

"You haven't touched your dinner," Malarchy complained. "Not eating isn't going to help."

"Nothing is going to help," Jade replied, pushing her mashed potatoes into the form of a mountain. She poured a vegetable-based gravy over top, allowing it to run down the sides. Her fork clanged on the plate, disappointed with the sculpture. "Waiting and not knowing is going to drive me crazy."

"That is exactly why it has been used as a tactic in many a war," Malarchy explained. "Living our lives, worrying about when or if isn't living at all."

"I can't help it," Jade argued. "We are losing parts of our team by the day. Those remaining feel disconnected. Are we even strong enough to take on another battle?"

Malarchy wiped his mouth with a white napkin before tossing it on the table. "We have to believe we are. How about some dessert? " He glanced around the restaurant. "Where in the realms did everyone go?" He stood. His voice dropped to a whisper. "Jade... your wand."

A blast sent Malarchy flying across the room. His body hit a wall and slid down into a hunched over pile. Jade ran to his side.

"There is a back room," he muttered, spewing out spots of blood. "Barricade yourself inside."

"Not without you," Jade squealed. A blast of green light escaped the tip of her wand, lifting her father's broken body.

"Come out. Come out," a voice cackled. "Wherever you are. I know I hit someone. Ah! There you are! I see you!"

"Who are you?!" Jade cried. "What do you want?"

An evil grin formed over pouting lips. "I am hurt you don't know my name." Her wand tapped against the palm of one hand. "I guess it doesn't really matter. I am Drakondia and I am here to avenge the fallen."

"The fallen?!" Jade exclaimed, glancing over her shoulder at the only path to survival. "Could you be a bit more explicit?" A few steps backward accompanied her words.

"Lucinda!" Drakondia screamed.

Jade covered her ears, the shrill sound of the woman's voice threatening to burst her eardrums. "I don't know who that is!" she yelled back.

"The Organization," Malarchy mumbled amidst coughs. "She was lust's victim."

Jade glanced at her father, then back at the task at hand. "We aren't to blame," she blurted out.

"I beg to differ," Drakondia said, her forked tongue leaving a layer of moisture on her lips. "You killed her and set my anger a blaze. The only way to put out such infernal pain is to release my wrath on those who caused it."

Jade's lips trembled. "That was Morynx," she blurted out, tears streaking down her cheeks. "There is a camp..."

"I have already been there and extracted the information I needed from the one you call a god," Drakondia interrupted. "I am done gathering information."

"Wait," Jade insisted. "Morynx is using you as a puppet. I can prove it. You recently felt a pinch somewhere on your body. There is a picture in that exact spot you didn't have before. That is the mark of the emotion sent to control you. In your case; wrath."

Drakondia howled a chilling laugh. Her wand pointed to a circular tattoo with a lion in its centre. "You mean this?" she hissed. A single finger caressed her own tattoo. The three dimensional spider began to move, crawling from just above her breast to the foreign branding on her arm. Fangs extended, piercing into the circle. A red coloured smoke wafted upward, forming a mini tornado before dissipating completely.

Jade shook her head. "I don't understand."

"The so-called puppet was merely a hitchhiker I used for directions," Drakondia explained. "We were heading the same way and had the same purpose, but I was always the one in charge." She cackled. "Wrath already resides in my soul. It doesn't need any help from the likes of Morynx. It only needs to be released."

Drakondia's wand pointed forward. A burst of energy flew from its tip. Father and daughter propelled backward, hitting another wall. The storage room door slammed behind them. Jade's wand pointed at the only way in or out.

"Don't bother with illusions," Malarchy ordered. "She'll see right through them. Put all your energy into a magical barricade. Hopefully, someone will find us before your energy expires."

"Toby!" Jade screamed.

"Aye, lass. I'm right here," the leprechaun replied. "There be no need to yell." He alternated glances between Jade and her father. "Oh."

"There is someone out there and I am no match for her." She watched her father, struggling to keep his eyes open. "I wish," Jade paused. "I wish for you to defeat our enemy!"

"Alas," Toby replied. "That is one wish I cannot fulfill. It is beyond my abilities."

"What?!" Jade shrieked. "I finally want to use a wish and you say no?! What good is that?"

"I am sorry, lass," Toby said. "I regret not being able to grant what you ask, but I told ye there were rules. I am bound to abide by them, like it or not."

"We are going to die in a storage room." Jade's hand quivered, the stream of magic faltering. "If you can't help us, I doubt there is anyone with enough power to."

"No," Toby announced. "You will not die here. Do not give up." He snapped his fingers, disappearing in a puff of green smoke.

Malarchy coughed up a mouthful of blood. "Remind me to never save a leprechaun."

Jade scooted over to his side. One hand intertwined with her father's while the other held the stream of magic flowing. She licked her lips, feeling them drying under the strain of energy depletion. It wouldn't be long before her manna was completely spent.

Toby reappeared, sending Joseph and Simon tumbling onto the floor before him. "I found some help."

"What happened?" Simon asked, taking Malarchy's free hand. "He's in bad shape. He needs a medical team. Toby, teleport him out."

"No!" Malarchy exclaimed. "I am not leaving my daughter. She needs the help."

"You also aren't doing much good in your condition," Simon replied.

"Neither am I without my wand," Joseph complained. "I'm little more than a sitting duck." He tossed the puzzle in the air with one hand.

"Give it to me," Jade demanded, catching it on the way back down. "I'll figure it out if I have to lose all my fingers."

"No," Toby said. He reached out and touched the box. The individual parts moved under his command, grinding louder than stone on stone. The noise came to an eerie halt. The puzzle popped open. "Take your prize, prince."

Joseph grasped the shaft of his wand. "Do we know who we are fighting?" he asked. "I guess it doesn't matter much. Let go of the barricade and I'll take over."

Jade glanced to her father for approval. A blink was enough of a confirmation to pull back. With Jade's magic released, the door flew open, splintering into toothpicks from the force on the opposite side. Simon held up one hand. The tiny projectiles stopped mid-flight, falling into a neat pile on the floor.

"Giving up so soon?" Drakondia cackled.

"We're just getting warmed up," Joseph replied, a coy smile gracing his lips.

Confidence oozed from his aura, spilling over in the form of sparks erupting from his eyes. The former prince took a few steps forward, his smile growing with each one.

"What do we have here?" Drakondia hissed. "A little boy playing hero?"

"I'm no boy," Joseph argued, "and I am certainly no hero. I owe these two a debt for some past... indiscretions."

Drakondia chuckled, moving a few paces closer. "Do you have it in you to kill, boy?"

Joseph pursed his lips together. A magical baton twirled in the air, landing with precision, the shaft in his palm. Instantly a stream of black light exploded, hitting Drakondia directly in her midsection.

"I think I can manage," Joseph snickered, preparing for a second attack, flanked by Simon and Jade.

Jade's eyes dazzled, set a glow with emerald flames. "Aim for the head," she ordered, nerves unwavering.

Two black streams bonded, forming a ribbon intertwined with a single green stripe layered between. Drakondia took aim, concentrating all of her defences directly in its path, but at the last second, it unraveled before her widening eyes. Each burst of magic attacked from a different angle; a direct hit from all fronts.

"No!" Drakondia screamed, her face shrivelling in defeat. She chose laughter for her final breath. "This is only the beginning. Revenge now falls to another, but I leave these realms knowing it will come and there is nothing you can do about it."

Her head mutated, becoming nothing more than an oversized stress ball. The final squeeze proved to be too much. Bulging eyes popped first, followed by an explosion that painted the walls in blood.

"Well," Joseph said, "that was rather messy. I don't think she'll be back, though." A brush appeared in place of his wand, meticulously attempting to clean his jacket of all debris. "Someone owes me a new suit."

"I think a trip to the medical building might be in order," Simon suggested. "We can sort things out from there." His wand waved in a circle, summoning help to their location.

"How is he?" Jade asked, glancing down at her father. Tears begged for release, stinging her eyes a crimson colour.

"He took quite a blow," Simon replied, squatting beside the mayor. "Malarchy is a strong man, though. I am sure he will be fine."

"His daughter is strong as well," Joseph said, his back turned to them. "You had the glimmer in your eyes during that fight. I saw it."

"The glimmer?" Jade questioned. "What is that supposed to mean?" Her arms crossed over her chest, awaiting an insult.

"Relax," Joseph said, without so much as a peek in her direction. "It is a good thing. It means your magic is capable of great feats. Not everyone finds their spark."

"I don't understand," Jade admitted. "What is it?"

Joseph laughed. "It happens at the exact moment you believe in yourself; you know you can do something and nothing can stop you. A flame ignites in your soul, displayed through windows."

"The eyes," Jade muttered.

"Exactly," Joseph agreed. "I know it well. Many a time the philosophy has served me in the past... succeed or be worthy of death's grip. No fear can live in the heart of the truly gifted."

"Would you have laid down your life just now?" Jade questioned.

"Had a creature like that bested me," Joseph snickered, "life wouldn't have been worth living." He turned to meet Jade's gaze. "Sometimes we all need to have faith in ourselves. That is the magic that actually does battle. Inner strength is always on the winning team. That is a lesson worth learning."

Jade watched her father being lifted by a stretcher. "Perhaps we can continue our conversation at the hospital."

"I'm afraid not," Joseph replied. "This is where our paths separate, at least for the moment. Thank your leprechaun for freeing my wand for me."

"Where are you going?" Jade asked.

"To find my sister, of course," Joseph answered. "Tell Prudance I'll contact her upon my return."

"It's dangerous!" Jade exclaimed.

"Only for those who believe it is," Joseph chuckled. Shoving one hand in his pocket, he strolled off.

Jade felt a hand on her shoulder. She glanced back at Simon shaking his head.

"Let him go," Simon said. "He has to try. I understand what he is feeling."

"He could die," Jade mumbled.

"He could," Simon agreed. "But better to die fighting for someone he loves than to wither away inside from doing nothing. If it was your family, wouldn't you attempt a rescue?"

"There is little hope," Jade replied.

"But there is some," Simon argued. "As long as the match is lit, he will continue looking. He is prepared to let it singe his fingertips. That was why he so desperately wanted his wand."

"I think I understand," Jade admitted.

# Chapter Fifteen

One minute all was normal, and the stars were shining down on the camp; the next, an eerie shadow swooped in and changed everything. On an eve of a new moon, light was already in short supply. The four vampires glanced at each other then up. The black clouds nightmares were made of blanketed the sky.

Their campfire crackled warnings of looming danger before being silenced to a mere ember glow. The calm before the storm set in. Less than a minute later, a different scene unfolded led by strong vibrations.

Gavin froze on the spot, his senses overloaded by chaos. The others weren't fairing much better. Safety was all that mattered -- not the equipment -- not the research. There was nothing like a natural disaster to bring out one's true colours. Which was more important, making it through still having a job, or self-preservation?

This quake was larger than the past ones had been. The earth literally came alive, rumbling with a ravenous hunger. The beast's belly demanded to be fed, cracking the ground beneath their feet, teasing the consequences if it wasn't.

"Is everyone okay?" Gavin yelled, his arms outstretched for additional balance. He waited for an answer from his three team members before attempting to move.

"This isn't a good sign," Russ said. "If we are turned upside down out here, I wonder how Kasper's team fared in there." He nodded at the cavern.

Gavin glanced from his right-hand man to the mouth of the mountain; a gaping hole capable of swallowing an army. Tremors had not only shook his legs, but his mind as well. He'd forgotten about Kasper's team, and more importantly, that Majesta was still inside the cave. She instantly became his new priority. Before another word could be uttered, he dashed to see what damage had been done.

"I'll wait for you here," Naomi scoffed, holding her head. Blood flowed from a gash on the side, colouring her hair in a sticky coat of brownish red.

Gavin's own heart beat louder than any voice, leaving him oblivious to her words. There was no hesitation. He raced by the entrance and deep into the heart of the cavern.

"Majesta!" His voice echoed through the tunnels with no answer. The orange glow up ahead shone blindingly bright. Shielding his eyes with his arms, pushing forward in the search for the missing ancient artifacts specialist.

A shower of dirt and pebbles rained down. A larger piece loomed overhead, threatening to dislodge from the ceiling. His own well-being fell to the wayside. Majesta needed to be found. There was nothing logical about the intense emotions he was feeling, but they couldn't be ignored.

"Majesta," Gavin called out a second time, his voice laced with desperation.

A faint sputtering cough caught his attention. Up ahead he could barely make out a slender pair of legs, hidden among pieces of rubble. He tossed a small boulder from atop Majesta's chest, as if it were a mere stone skipping on the surface of a pond. Steady arms scooped up her bruised and battered body, carrying her to the safety of the camp's clearing.

Gavin placed the artifacts specialist down on the ground. With one ear on her chest, he listened to her heart beat. Hearing it thump was the most he could hope for. First aid wasn't required curriculum in the vampire school of hard knocks.

"I'm okay," Majesta whispered.

"Thank goodness," Gavin said, a sigh of relief acting as an exclamation point at the end of his words.

"The workers?" Majesta muttered, holding her head. "Are they okay?"

"I didn't see anyone else in there," Gavin replied, glancing back over his shoulder. "I'll take another look as soon as I am sure you are all right."

"Send one of the others," Majesta begged. "Stay with me here."

"I can't ask them to risk their lives for men they hate," Gavin replied. His lips pursed together, forming a thin line of indecision. "I should look for the men. One or more of them could be badly hurt. In which case, Kasper might pull the plug on your expedition."

Majesta nodded. "Do what you must. I'll wait here." Her gaze followed the vampire as his body disappeared and another came into view.

"You don't look hurt," Naomi scoffed, crouching down. Her head tilted from side to side. "No sign of blood. You'll have a few bruises, but with women like you that's just a part of the job. So what game are you playing?"

Majesta forced a smile. "I don't know what you mean. I was inside when the earthquake..."

Naomi let out the cackle of a mad woman. "Liar!" she screamed. "You like him, don't you?"

"Who?" Majesta asked.

"Don't toy with me," Naomi hissed, her face wrinkling under the strain of disdain. "Gavin! Let me give you a piece of advice. I was here first. He belongs with me. I'm watching every move you make." She motioned with two fingers. They alternated pointing between her own eyes and the ancient artifacts specialist's while she backtracked to a spot in front of the mountainside.

Gavin emerged moments later. His arm brushed Naomi's, but the bump didn't register. Her head tilted back as far as her neck would stretch, shaking in a silent tantrum.

"There is no sign of anyone," Gavin said.

"My research..."

Gavin held up one hand. "There isn't as much damage as I anticipated. It is mainly loose dirt and small rocks, all of which can easily be cleaned up."

"Thank goodness!" Majesta exclaimed.

"Yeah," Gavin mumbled. "It's odd, though. If the workers were in there, where did they go? There should be some sign of them left."

"Maybe they ran," Majesta suggested. "It was frightening. They could have headed for the hills, thinking everything was coming down."

"Maybe," Gavin said, rubbing his neck. "The quake probably knocked out our communications again. I may need to head to Pewterclaw to make sure they made it back."

"You?!" Majesta shrieked.

"Yeah," Gavin replied. "Why, is that a problem?"

Majesta reached for his hand. "With the other men gone, I have no protection against those who wish to keep the secrets of the mountain buried within it." She leaned forward, her lips grazing against his cheek. Her eyes locked on those of Naomi, still lurking a few hundred feet away.

"What was that for?" Gavin asked, a smile forming in his eyes before spreading to the rest of his face.

"I didn't thank you for going in to look for the rest of my team," Majesta answered. "No one else here would have done that for strangers. Perhaps, another member of your team could head to the city." She nodded toward the cave.

Gavin glanced over his shoulder. "Naomi," he muttered, rolling his eyes. He paused. "That might actually be a good idea. I think any one of the three could use a break from this place. It's driving us all a little mad. I'll talk to Russ and Delphine and see what they think. Whoever volunteers can head back. Don't go away. I'll be right back."

Naomi was by her side the moment Gavin left. "I thought I made it clear. He's mine."

Majesta glanced at the circular mark on the vampire's arm. "Shouldn't Gavin be the one to decide that?" she teased.

"You are living dangerously," Naomi replied through grinding teeth.

"Relax," Majesta said. "I have no interest in your man, nor he in me. In fact, I believe you were meant for each other." She paused, her lips twitching. "If it weren't for that green-eyed girl that is. She's the one in your way. He has all but admitted it to me in confidence."

"Jade!" Naomi exclaimed in disgust. "There isn't much I can do about the mayor's daughter from here, though."

"Gavin wants to send one of you three back to Pewterclaw," Majesta stated. "If it were you..."

"I could take care of that little witch once and for all." A wicked smile crept over her face. "With Jade gone, there will be no one left in my way."

"My thought's exactly," Majesta muttered.

# Chapter Sixteen

All of the beds in the medical ward were empty, save for the one Malarchy was lying in and another on the opposite side of the room. That one was being occupied by Prudance's mother.

"You need to go home and get some rest," Malarchy mumbled, his voice straining against the effects of drugs designed to induce sleep.

"I will," Jade said, lifting their finger-intertwined hands to her lips. "As soon as I am sure you are going to be okay."

"I'm fine," Malarchy replied. "A little rest and I will be as good as new. I promise."

Jade's eyes went dull. "She was more powerful than the puppet. How is that possible?"

Malarchy sighed. "Not her," he explained. "The sins are all strong emotions. From what we know, Morynx commands them to find an easy target, someone who is predisposed to a particular sin. The puppets force each of their victims to feel the full extent of their allotted emotion. In Drakondia's case, however, she was already consumed by wrath. Adding more was overkill."

"So you are saying her own rage was more powerful than the one commanded by Morynx," Jade mumbled.

"Yes," Malarchy agreed. "I believe that is how she dismissed the puppet so easily. Unfortunately, I think she may have pushed the dial forward at the same time. If it left believing its job was successfully completed..."

"Then we are on to a new sin," Jade said. "There aren't many left and we still don't know what happens when they are all gone."

"We may not ever know..." Malarchy's words faded.

"Until we lose," Jade said, ending his thoughts. "It's okay. I am starting to wonder if we ever had a chance."

"Our list of allies is growing thin," Malarchy groaned. "I am bedridden for a few days; Stan and Miss Kelly aren't back yet from training; and Esmerelda is still hiding Kasper from us.

You'll need to be very careful. Round up those remaining. There is safety in numbers."

"Luckily," Toby interrupted, "Ye still have me by yer side and I'm sticking like glue."

Malarchy rolled his eyes. "No wishes!" he ordered. "That's the last thing she needs right now."

"That's right!" Jade exclaimed. "I used a wish and nothing bad happened!"

"Not exactly," Toby replied.

"What do you mean?" Malarchy barked. "I vaguely remember hearing her make the wish myself."

"Aye," Toby agreed, taking a seat on Jade's shoulder. "So she did." A frown crossed his lips. "As it be, I wasn't able to grant said wish."

"At first," Jade argued, "you declined because you didn't think you could defeat the enemy, but then you brought back Simon and Joseph to do it."

"I brought them back of me own free will," Toby explained. "Ye didn't wish for that."

"What about the puzzle box?" Jade questioned. "You opened it for me."

"Technically I opened it for me," Toby answered. "Ye never asked me to. I solved it because I couldn't bear the thought of lovely fingers being snapped at by crocodile teeth. It brought a tear to me eye."

"The only crocodile here is the one crying those tears," Malarchy complained. "What's in it for you?"

"Nothing," Toby snapped. "Except the satisfaction of knowing your lovely daughter wasn't hurt. I can't guarantee the same will be said for the final three sins, though. These trials are becoming more difficult."

"It's not like there is much we can do about that," Jade said. "They are going to come no matter what. Whatever the game Morynx started, I believe we are bound to see through to the end."

"You are a smart lass," Toby said. "Looks like the excitement finally caught up to pops." He motioned to Malarchy fast asleep. "It's time for you to do the same. You'll be needing ye rest come daybreak. At least take the bed over yonder and have a bit of a wee lie down. I'll keep watch for this one eve."

Jade nodded her agreement. "Toby," she said, "are you staying through all of it? It would be nice to know I have someone in my corner at the very end."

"Aye, lass," Toby answered. "I am."

The sheets lifted, covering Jade's body after she lay down. Sleep took her as soon as her head hit the pillow.

"I have no choice in the matter," Toby whispered. "I wish there was another way. Sleep well, my sweet Jade. For in the morning, a new threat will be waiting yer pretty eyes."

# Author's Message

I hope you enjoyed reading *Wrath* as much as I did writing it.

There is much more to come in the Surviving the Sins saga. Watch for *Envy*, coming soon.

Until next time... happy reading!

# ABOUT THE AUTHOR

C.A. King is the recipient of several awards, including: The Hamilton Spectator Readers' Choice Award for 2017 & 2018 Best Author; The Brant News Readers' Choice Award for 2017 Best Author; Readers' Favorite award in the short story/novella category; the 2017 SIBA Award for Best New Adult; the 2017 SIBA Award for Best Novella; 2018 Readers' Favorite International Book Awards: Gold Medal in the Fiction - Supernatural genre; and 2018 Readers' Favorite International Book Awards: Bronze Medal in the Fiction - New Adult genre

Currently residing in Brantford, Ontario Canada, she lives with her two sons. She began her writing career after the tragic loss of her parents and husband. Redirecting her emotions through writing became therapeutic in her battle with depression and in 2014 she decided to publish some of her works.

# Other Titles from C.A. King

## The Portal Prophecies

These great titles in C.A. King's The Portal Prophecies series are available now at most online book retailers:

*A Keeper's Destiny*

*A Halloween's Curse*

*Frost Bitten*

*Sleeping Sands*

*Deadly Perceptions*

*Finding Balance*

*Volume I (Books 1-3)*

*Volume II (Books 4-6)*

The prophecies are the key to their survival. Can they solve them in time?

## Shattering the Effects of Time

Join the Shinning brothers, Jessie, Dezi and Pete as they set out on a quest to save their younger sister. No magic known to them or their friends has ever been able to reverse the grip of time. A few legends, however, exist mentioning ancient items that may hold the key to do exactly that.

This brand new series will take you on a search for the Fountain of Youth and Mermaids; a quest for the Holy Grail; a trip to visit Daryl the mountain guru, in the hunt for the Cinamani Stone; on a search for Ambrosia, the food of the Gods; and other adventures.

## *Surviving the Sins: Answering the Call*

The prophecies are being rewritten. This time someone is using the seven deadly sins: Lust; Gluttony; Greed; Sloth; Wrath; Envy; and Pride, to unlock an ancient evil. The book falls into Jade's hands to answer destiny's call. Can she survive the sins?

## *Surviving the Sins: Pride*

No one is safe when a witch's pride is at stake.

Prudance is back in Pewterclaw, and she isn't about to give up her prestigious status without a fight - especially not because of vampires. As an eighth-generation witch, she plans to do whatever it takes to stop the proposed new legislation from becoming law, including waking the dead for help.

Humility isn't in her vocabulary. With an ego spinning out of control and ancestral power at her fingertips, Prudance weaves a plot to keep Jade and Gavin separated. Will it be enough to satisfy the spirits she summoned?

When her pride costs more than she bargained for, someone has to pay the tab - but who will it be?

## *Surviving the Sins: Lust*

What Mother doesn't know won't hurt her.

Lucinda has spent her entire existence running The Organization and looking after Mother's needs without complaint. That's about to change. A burning desire had manifested inside her - one she could no longer deny... Lust.

When Constable Safron Black shows up unexpected with news of an imprisoned God, Lucinda unravels. With power fuelling her passion, she'll do anything to make Morynx her mate.

**********

Jade and her friends find themselves at a standstill. They have already failed to stop Pride from completing its task and they haven't located any victims for the other six sins. A strange fire in the municipal office puts them hot on the trail of what could be answers. Will they be in time to stop the dial from moving and further opening the way for Morynx?

## Gluttony

Zoe never claimed to be the virtuous type; her lack of patience was proof of that. The transition from princess to barmaid never sat well with her. Without a wand, however, there was little she could do to change things.

In one fleeting moment, her universe was turned upside down. The answer to all her problems was staring her in the face from within her brother's grasp. With control of one tiny vial, she would have her cake and everyone else's too. Turning her back on family was a small price to pay in comparison.

Joseph mentioned once that being a glutton didn't suit her. With an abundance of newfound power, she intended to prove him wrong.

## *When Leaves Fall: A Different Point of View Story*

Ralph wakes up to what others only experience in a nightmare. Chained to a shed, he has no idea where he is, or who his captor is. His memories a blurred at best. As the days press on he finds himself experiencing a roller coaster of feelings. Hunger, thirst and pain become his only companions. Flashbacks of a happier time are all he has to keep him going. As his situation deteriorates, he finds himself doubting the very things he wants most - a family.

*When Leaves Fall* is a dramatic-thriller with a twist. Keep the tissue box close for the ending.

## Tomoiya's Story

A Vampire Tale. She had a secret but she wasn't the only one who had something to hide.

Book I ~ Escape to Darkness

Book II ~ Collecting Tears

Book III~ Coming Soon

## Peach Coloured Daisies:

## A Cursed by the Gods Story

He couldn't die. An ancient curse meant she always did. This time, that was going to change - one way or another.

When Daisy's grandmother, her last living relative, passes away, she doesn't know where to turn. Things go from bad to worse when a local psychic tells her about a curse. Alone and confused, she ends up in front of her college professor's office, ready to cry her heart out in his arms.

Matt Demi might be the son of a God, but he's living the life of a cursed man. He's had to watch the woman he loves die on her twenty-first birthday countless times. Nothing he does seems to be able to affect the outcome. When she shows up at his office scared out of her wits by a psychic's prediction, he vows this time will be different.

With only three days, Matt will need to embrace a side of him he swore off long ago to save her, but will he lose himself in the process?

## Flower Shields: A Four Horsemen Novel

Meet the four horsemen: Michael, Gabrielle, Uriel and Raphael. For centuries their job has been to guard the gates of hell, making sure they never open. Without the keys, there was never any real threat. That's about to change. There are rumours on the horizon that demon followers unearthed scrolls that explain exactly how to find the lost keys. This new battle is a race to see which side locates them first.

Michael couldn't care less about the love story behind how and why the world was created. In fact, nothing matters to him other than keeping the gates to hell closed. If one of the lost keys ever fell into the wrong hands, all humanity would be doomed. He's not going to let that happen - at any cost.

**********

Tara's life is nothing short of a disaster. She's managed to flunk out of college with about the same amount of dignity as every relationship she's been in. The only constant in her life has been her love for flowers. When she's attacked at work, a stranger comes to her aid. Michael might be good-looking, but he's also arrogant, bossy and crazy. He's also her only chance to figure out who attacked her and why. Should she follow her heart and trust him - or listen to her head and run?

## *Drawing Strength From Words: A Four Horsemen Novel*

Meet the four horsemen: Michael, Gabrielle, Uriel and Raphael.

For centuries their sole purpose has been guarding the sealed gates to hell. Without keys, there was never any real threat. That was about to change...

For Gabrielle, protecting mankind was merely a job for which she received little credit. The vast insecurities of men altered history itself, portraying her as a masculine brute. Taking a back seat to her brothers seemed the right thing to do, but left a bitter taste in her mouth and an impenetrable barricade shielding her heart.

**********

Ryder bounced around the system from the moment both his parents were killed. Between that and run-ins with the law for crimes he never committed, it seemed the whole world was conspiring against him. Never growing attached to anyone was rule number one: a rule he'd never broken until a white-haired vixen, with blocks of ice on her shoulders, walked right into his life. Melting through those frosty layers became all that mattered, even if that meant sacrificing himself in the process.

## *Miracles Not Included*

A heartfelt romantic story about: life; love; loss; and learning to love again. If only life came with instructions and a warning label ~ Miracles Not Included.

**********

Chris was born to be a writer. Even the smallest of details couldn't pass without notice, often becoming part of a plot for her next novel. The one thing she never saw coming was her husband's sudden illness.

Jason loved his wife from the moment they met. Nothing could ever change that - nothing except the death sentence he'd been handed - a terminal cancer diagnosis.

His story was ending: Hers was starting a new chapter and more than one miracle was needed to turn the page.

## Twisted Tales of a Dead End Street

A paranormal mystery laced with comedic undertones: Twisted Tales of a Dead End Street.

Nine neighbours were invited to the mysterious dinner party at 9 Nine Street. Their host, the owner of the mansion, had more planned for the evening than just roast beef.

When the secret of their quiet street was revealed, everything changed, blurring the lines between the tangible and the paranormal.

Was the number nine the difference between life and death? Would any of them survive long enough to uncover the truth? They would each soon find out this wasn't a simple case of who-done-it so much as one of what was being done and by whom.

## Shot Through The Heart: A Faerie Tale

A tale of two worlds - one filled with magic; the other void of it. But what happened to those trapped between the two? Adelia was about to find out...

Magic and structure were the foundations of her existence. Temptation controlled the ability to destroy everything she knew. The world of men held a powerful allure over her heart, waking that which had long been dormant. It enticed her, snagging her in a web of emotions.

A decision had to be made. Was feeling love for the first time worth sacrificing magic and immortality?

## Do Not Open Until Halloween

When eighteen year old Caitlin agreed to babysit her eccentric Aunt's two cats and house, she had no idea that Justin was finally going to ask her for a date the same weekend. Torn between family and crush, she chose to take her best friends' suggestion to heart, arranging a small Friday night gathering. Little did she know a fairy was about to crash the party with trouble hot on her wings.

Caitlin will have to dig deep to find even a smidgen of belief in magic or there won't be any hope of saving her new friend from being hunted.

In this young adult fantasy, award-winning author, C.A. King, explores the answer to one of the questions readers have always wanted to ask...

Where do fairies come from?

### *Truly Unfortunate*

Growing up in Knoll County wasn't easy, especially without any childhood memories. Truly spent her whole life searching for the answers her mind refused to reveal. There might have been horrors in her past, but her current existence wasn't much better than a nightmare. After beginning treatments with a new doctor, disturbing visions began to resurface. The stench of death surrounded her, but where exactly was it coming from?

Jeff always knew he wanted to be one of Knoll County's finest and had no problem achieving that dream. A part of his ambition stemmed from the death of a classmate at the tender age of nine. It might have been ruled an accident, but his gut told him otherwise. When people start turning up dead in the same pattern, Jeff will be forced to put everything on the line to connect the dots between past and present. But in doing so, will his own future be jeopardized?

Truly Unfortunate is a dark paranormal thriller that will leave readers with chills after answering the question: Which is stronger... the boundaries of reality or the safety on one's own mind?

### *Merry Apocalypse*

For centuries, families gathered throughout the holiday season to hear recitals of the famous words of Dr. Clement C. Moore's 'Twas the Night Before Christmas and celebrate the long awaited return of Santa. His jovial generosity became synonymous with all that was Merry and bright. Then everything changed.

This year, the gatherings are sharing their own Christmas story. Merry Apocalypse includes the telling of a new traditional tale that echoes the tone and rhythm of familiar poetry, but instead of joy and bliss, contains warnings of danger and death.

### Sometimes Love Stinks

What's in a name? Everything when it's laughable.

Gastrella M. Balance was living a never-ending nightmare. For several years, she'd been the butt of jokes about... her butt. Moving to Knollville was a chance for a fresh start. It was a place where no one knew her past, or her name and she was determined to keep both a secret. Her strategy was to stay under the radar and as inconspicuous as possible. That plan, however, went south the first time she laid eyes on Tanner. When he noticed her, too, she couldn't help but hope for a bit of romance, no matter how far fetched it seemed.

*****

Tanner had everything a guy could ask for in his senior year of high school. He had a football in one hand and a pretty girl hanging off the other arm. Being popular and the centre of attention came naturally to him. Taking tests, however, did not and he was desperate to keep that part of his life to himself.

When a series of pranks go awry, they'll both be faced with confronting their personal anxieties. Together, they might have a chance to overcome the odds and survive the year.

Sometimes Love Stinks is a romantic comedy that deals with issues that are both real and difficult. While the main characters in this story are from the mundane world, readers can expect to find the signature supernatural kiss C.A. King adds to all her books.